The Curse of the Gingerbread Golem

The Curse of the Gingerbread Golem

Matthew Petchinsky

The Curse of the Gingerbread Golem
By: Matthew Petchinsky

Introduction: A Town on the Edge

Nestled in the heart of a snow-covered valley, the quaint town of Frostwood seemed to embody the very essence of holiday cheer. Its streets, lined with cobblestone and flanked by Victorian-style houses, were adorned with twinkling lights and garlands that glittered in the frosty air. Wreaths hung on every door, carolers practiced their songs, and the scent of freshly baked gingerbread wafted through the town square, mingling with the crisp, pine-scented breeze.

At the center of it all was the annual Gingerbread Festival, a tradition as old as the town itself. For as long as anyone could remember, the festival had marked the start of the holiday season, drawing visitors from neighboring towns and even a few out-of-state tourists. Frostwood's claim to fame was its life-sized gingerbread displays: houses, figures, and fantastical sculptures, each painstakingly crafted by the local bakers and assembled in the square. The pièce de résistance was always the grand gingerbread man—a towering confection that symbolized unity, joy, and the spirit of the season.

Yet, beneath the town's picture-perfect exterior, there was an unease that the festive decorations couldn't mask. It began subtly at first: a dog barking furiously at the empty square after sundown, a child claiming to hear whispers coming from the gingerbread house display, and the bakery's delivery boy swearing he saw shadows move in the early morning fog. Though dismissed as nerves or holiday excitement, these small incidents planted seeds of doubt in the hearts of the townsfolk.

Frostwood had always been a town deeply connected to its past, and its traditions were more than mere customs—they were rituals, carried out with reverence. The Gingerbread Festival was no exception. Legend had it that the festival began over two centuries ago, during the town's harshest winter on record. According to local lore, the settlers faced starvation after their crops failed and their livestock perished. In desperation, they turned to the ancient art of gingerbread baking, believed to have protective and even mystical properties. Their offerings were baked not just as sustenance but as a plea for survival, crafted with intricate designs and imbued with intentions of hope and unity.

Miraculously, the settlers survived that winter, and from then on, the festival became a yearly tradition. Over time, the true origins of the ritual faded into folklore, and the story became more about resilience than desperation. Few remembered the darker elements of the tale: the whispers of a curse tied to the festival, the warnings etched into the margins of old recipe books, and the unexplained disappearances that punctuated the town's history.

This year, the festival promised to be grander than ever. Clara Simmons, a young and ambitious baker, had taken charge of the preparations, determined to revive some of the older, forgotten traditions. She'd spent weeks pouring over Mrs. Hannigan's recipe archives, rediscovering forgotten techniques and flavors. Her enthusiasm was infectious, and the townsfolk rallied around her vision, eager to see Frostwood outshine its previous festivals.

But Clara's passion blinded her to the warnings hidden within those dusty pages. Mrs. Hannigan, the town's aging matriarch and keeper of its culinary history, had tried to caution her. "Some recipes are better left forgotten," she'd said cryptically, her voice trembling. Clara had laughed it off, assuming the old woman was simply resistant to change. After all, what harm could a little tradition do?

As the festival drew closer, the unease in Frostwood deepened. The weather, usually mild for the season, turned bitterly cold. Frost etched strange patterns onto windows, resembling skeletal trees and clawed hands. Livestock began acting erratically—dogs refused to enter the square, and horses spooked at the sound of distant bells. More unsettling were the reports from the children:

they spoke of seeing a "gingerbread man" lurking near the bakery, its eyes glowing faintly in the dark.

By the night before the festival, the town square was a dazzling display of holiday magic. The grand gingerbread man, standing nearly eight feet tall, took its place at the center of the festivities, its frosting smile seeming almost lifelike. Clara stood back to admire her work, brushing off the odd feeling that its gumdrop eyes were watching her. The townsfolk gathered for a brief ceremony, cheering as the mayor declared the festival officially open.

But as the crowd dispersed, and the square grew quiet, something shifted. The festive air seemed to grow heavy, the scents of sugar and spice turning cloying and oppressive. A strange hush fell over the town, broken only by the faint sound of cracking—like ice breaking underfoot or dough stretching in an oven. It came from the direction of the grand gingerbread man.

Unbeknownst to Clara and the rest of Frostwood, their beloved tradition had awakened something ancient and vengeful. The holiday cheer that once defined their town would soon give way to a nightmare they could never have imagined. The curse of the Gingerbread Golem had begun to stir.

Chapter 1: The Legend in the Dough

The scent of cinnamon and cloves filled the air as Clara swept the flour-covered floor of Hannigan's Bakery. It was a cozy place, with its well-worn wooden countertops, shelves lined with jars of spices and extracts, and a brick oven that seemed ancient enough to have stories of its own. Clara had been working there for years, first as an apprentice and now as a skilled baker, but tonight she felt like a child again as she sat across from Mrs. Hannigan by the flickering light of the bakery's hearth.

Mrs. Hannigan, the town's oldest resident, was as much a fixture of Frostwood as the festival itself. Her hands, gnarled with age and arthritis, still moved deftly as she kneaded dough and shaped pastries with an artistry that seemed almost magical. She was known for her stories, and as the night stretched on, Clara knew the elder baker had one ready—a tale that would chill the bones despite the warmth of the room.

The old woman's voice, hoarse and measured, carried a weight of authority as she began. "You know, Clara, every tradition has its roots. And not all of them are as sweet as the icing on a gingerbread cookie. The Gingerbread Festival you love so much—it started long before this town was about Christmas cheer and holiday lights. It was born out of desperation. Fear."

Clara paused her sweeping, captivated. Mrs. Hannigan rarely spoke about the festival's origins beyond the surface-level pleasantries the town peddled to tourists. Tonight, though, there was a gravity in her tone, an urgency that made Clara set her broom aside and sit down to listen.

"It was the winter of 1783," Mrs. Hannigan began. "The settlers who founded Frostwood were struggling. The cold came early that year, harsher than anyone had prepared for. Crops failed, food stores dwindled, and the snow piled so high it buried entire cabins. Wolves prowled the outskirts of town, and there was talk of raiders—bands of men who wouldn't hesitate to kill for a loaf of bread."

Clara shivered, pulling her apron tighter around her. She had heard stories of Frostwood's harsh winters before, but Mrs. Hannigan's voice painted the scene with visceral clarity.

"The town's leaders, desperate to protect what little they had left, turned to a woman named Margery Grimmel—a baker with knowledge of the old ways. She was no ordinary woman; the people whispered that her recipes weren't just for food but for something more. Margery claimed she could bake protection, craft life from the elements of her trade. She offered to create a guardian for the town—a golem, baked from gingerbread, brought to life with a ritual that would bind it to the town's safety."

Clara leaned in, her heart racing. "A gingerbread golem?" she echoed.

Mrs. Hannigan nodded solemnly. "The golem was to be a silent protector, standing watch over the town. Margery baked it from a special dough, enriched with the town's last reserves of sugar, molasses, and spices. But it wasn't just the ingredients that gave it power. Margery added something else—something dark. She claimed the golem needed a 'heart' to give it purpose, to bind it to its task."

Clara's voice dropped to a whisper. "A heart?"

The old baker's eyes glistened in the firelight. "A child," she said gravely. "Margery took an orphan boy, a child no one would miss, and used his spirit to animate the dough. The ritual worked—the golem rose, eight feet tall, with eyes of frosted sugar and claws of jagged icing. It drove off the wolves, scared away the raiders, and protected the town through the worst of the winter."

Clara felt a chill that had nothing to do with the cold outside. "But... if it saved the town, why is it a legend people don't talk about?"

Mrs. Hannigan's hands stilled over the dough she had been kneading. "Because the golem didn't stop with the raiders. It grew restless. The child's spirit inside it was angry, confused. Instead of protecting the town, it turned on the very people it was meant to serve. Houses burned, livestock were slaughtered, and people vanished—dragged into the forest by a creature they could no longer control. Margery tried to destroy it, but it was too late. The golem tore her apart and rampaged through Frostwood until the townsfolk banded together to trap it."

Clara felt her pulse quicken. "Trap it? How?"

"They lured it to the edge of the forest, to a clearing where they had prepared a massive kiln. They tricked it inside, locking it in with chains, and set the kiln ablaze. The townsfolk thought they had destroyed it, but Margery's dying words warned them: 'As long as the spirit remains unatoned, the golem cannot truly be destroyed.'"

The room fell silent, the only sound the faint crackle of the fire. Clara's throat felt dry as she processed the story. "So... you're saying the golem could come back?"

Mrs. Hannigan looked at her with a gaze that seemed to pierce right through her. "Legends have a way of lingering, Clara. The golem's spirit is bound to the recipe Margery used, and as long as that recipe exists, so does the curse. Every year, the festival brings together the same ingredients: flour, molasses, sugar, spice... and intention. That's all it needs to rise again. You've been digging into old recipes, haven't you?"

Clara's heart sank. "I—yes, but I didn't know—"

The old woman cut her off. "You've awakened something, girl. Be careful with what you bake. The Gingerbread Festival may be a celebration, but it's also a ritual. And rituals have consequences."

As the fire flickered lower and the shadows in the bakery grew longer, Clara couldn't shake the feeling that something—or someone—was watching her from the darkness. Mrs. Hannigan's words echoed in her mind, and for the first time, the sweet scent of gingerbread turned her stomach.

Chapter 2: The Unveiling

The early morning light streamed through the frosted windows of Hannigan's Bakery, casting golden rays over rows of neatly arranged pastries and jars of spices. Clara had been cleaning out the storage room, a task Mrs. Hannigan had been avoiding for decades. Dust motes danced in the air as she worked, pulling out old sacks of flour, rusted cookie cutters, and faded recipe cards.

"Why does she keep all this junk?" Clara muttered, coughing as a cloud of flour puffed into her face.

"Because junk, as you call it, often holds history," Mrs. Hannigan replied from the doorway, startling Clara. The old woman's sharp eyes swept the room. "Careful with what you throw away. Some things are better left forgotten."

Clara rolled her eyes, though she tried to hide it. "I'm just trying to clear some space. This room hasn't been touched in years."

Mrs. Hannigan's gaze lingered on an old wooden chest tucked into the corner. Its iron latch was rusted shut, and the wood was scarred with deep gouges, as if something had tried to claw its way in—or out.

"You won't find anything useful in there," Mrs. Hannigan said quickly, her tone sharper than usual. "Leave it be."

Clara's curiosity piqued. "What's in it?"

"Nothing you need," Mrs. Hannigan snapped. "Focus on what you were hired to do, Clara. The festival's in two days, and we have orders to fill."

With that, the old woman turned and shuffled back toward the front of the bakery, her cane tapping against the floorboards. Clara watched her go, then glanced back at the chest. Mrs. Hannigan's warning only made her more determined to open it.

Hours later, when Mrs. Hannigan had left for her afternoon tea with the mayor's wife, Clara returned to the storage room armed with a crowbar. She hesitated for a moment, Mrs. Hannigan's words replaying in her mind. But curiosity won out.

The latch gave way with a loud crack, and the chest creaked open. Inside was a single object: a thick, leather-bound recipe book. Its cover was embossed with strange symbols, some resembling runes, others looking like curling vines. The pages were yellowed with age, and the edges were brittle.

"Whoa," Clara whispered, lifting the book carefully. She carried it to the counter and flipped it open. The handwriting was old-fashioned, looping and ornate, with occasional notes scribbled in the margins. The recipes were unlike anything Clara had seen before—some called for ingredients like "star anise from the winter's first frost" or "sugar ground under a waxing moon."

As she turned the pages, one recipe caught her eye. It was titled "The Guardian's Gingerbread: A Protector Bound by Spice and Spirit." Beneath the title was an illustration of a massive gingerbread figure, its eyes glowing like coals and its jagged teeth set in a wicked grin.

Clara read the ingredients aloud, a smile creeping onto her face. "Flour, molasses, cinnamon... this doesn't seem so different from a regular gingerbread recipe."

But the notes scribbled in the margins gave her pause. "Beware the balance of intention."
"Do not invoke the heart without caution."
"Only the worthy may command its power."

"Command its power?" Clara said with a laugh. "It's gingerbread, not a magic spell."

Ignoring the warnings, Clara copied the recipe onto a fresh sheet of paper and began gathering the ingredients. She wasn't superstitious, and the thought of presenting such a grand gingerbread man at the festival thrilled her. It would be a showstopper, a centerpiece unlike anything Frostwood had seen in years.

The kitchen was a flurry of activity as Clara mixed the dough. The recipe called for an unusually high amount of molasses, which gave the dough a rich, dark color. She added a blend of spices—cinnamon, ginger, cloves, and nutmeg—and marveled at the intoxicating aroma. It smelled deeper, almost primal, compared to her usual gingerbread.

As she rolled out the dough, Clara found herself humming a tune she didn't recognize. It was low and lilting, almost like a chant. She shook her head, brushing it off as her imagination.

After hours of work, the massive gingerbread man was ready for the oven. It stood nearly eight feet tall, its limbs thick and sturdy. Clara had used dried cranberries for the eyes and licorice whips for its mouth. She decorated its chest with swirling patterns of icing, mimicking the intricate designs in the recipe's illustration.

"This is going to be incredible," she said aloud, stepping back to admire her work. She slid the tray into the bakery's industrial oven, setting the timer and leaning against the counter with a satisfied sigh.

The first sign that something was wrong came about halfway through the baking. The air in the kitchen grew heavy, the sweet aroma of gingerbread taking on a cloying, almost suffocating quality. The oven emitted strange noises—popping and crackling, followed by what sounded like a low growl.

Clara frowned. "Is the fan acting up again?" she muttered, opening the oven door slightly to peek inside.

A wave of heat blasted her face, accompanied by a strange, almost metallic scent. The gingerbread man's surface seemed to shimmer, as if it were alive. For a moment, Clara thought she saw one of its cranberry eyes move, but she shook her head, blaming the heat.

She closed the oven quickly, her heart racing. "Get a grip, Clara," she told herself. "It's just a batch of gingerbread."

When the timer dinged, she carefully pulled the tray out of the oven. The gingerbread man was perfect—or so it seemed. Its surface was smooth and golden-brown, its eyes gleaming unnervingly in the dim kitchen light.

Clara reached for her piping bag to add the final touches, but as she leaned closer, she thought she heard something. It was faint, almost imperceptible, like a whisper.

"...free..."

She froze, her hand hovering over the tray. "What the hell?"

The whisper came again, clearer this time. "...release me..."

Clara stumbled back, nearly dropping the piping bag. Her breath came in short gasps as she stared at the gingerbread man. Its cranberries glistened wetly, and the licorice mouth seemed to curl upward into a grin.

"No," she whispered. "It's just the heat playing tricks on me."

But deep down, Clara knew something was wrong. Very wrong. And in her chest, a terrible realization began to grow: she had done something more than bake a gingerbread man. She had awakened something. Something ancient. Something hungry.

The kitchen lights flickered, and for the briefest moment, the towering gingerbread figure seemed to shift—its arm twitching ever so slightly. Clara blinked, and it was still again. But the oppressive feeling in the room remained, heavy and suffocating.

She turned off the lights and left the bakery in a hurry, telling herself it was just exhaustion. But as the door clicked shut behind her, she failed to notice the faint sound of cracking dough and the low, resonant hum of something stirring to life.

Chapter 3: The First Omen

The festival had arrived, and Frostwood's town square was transformed into a holiday wonderland. Twinkling lights draped every building, casting a golden glow over the bustling crowd. Children laughed as they played among the booths, where vendors sold steaming mugs of cider, handmade ornaments, and plates of sugar-dusted treats. The crisp air was alive with the sounds of carolers and the clinking of bells, but something about the festive atmosphere felt... strained.

At the center of it all stood the grand gingerbread man, towering over the square. Clara's creation was a marvel, a giant confection that seemed almost too perfect. Its cranberry eyes gleamed under the lights, its frosting design intricate and mesmerizing. Townsfolk gathered around it, snapping pictures and admiring Clara's handiwork.

"Clara, this is spectacular!" the mayor exclaimed, clapping her on the back. "This is the best centerpiece we've ever had."

Clara forced a smile. "Thanks, Mayor. I'm glad everyone likes it."

But inwardly, her stomach churned. She couldn't shake the unease that had settled over her since the night she'd baked the gingerbread man. The strange whispers, the flickering lights, the way its licorice grin seemed to curl wider when she wasn't looking—it had all left her feeling on edge. She told herself it was just nerves, the pressure of wanting the festival to be perfect. And yet...

"Are you all right, dear?" asked Mrs. Hannigan, appearing at Clara's side. The old woman's sharp eyes flicked to the gingerbread man, her expression unreadable.

"I'm fine," Clara lied. "Just a little tired."

Mrs. Hannigan frowned but said nothing. Instead, she studied the towering gingerbread figure, her lips pressed into a thin line. "You used it, didn't you?" she murmured so only Clara could hear.

Clara's heart skipped a beat. "Used what?"

"The recipe," Mrs. Hannigan said, her voice low and accusatory. "The one from the book. You should have left it alone."

Before Clara could respond, a child's shrill laughter broke through the crowd. A little girl, no older than six, ran toward the gingerbread man, her mittened hands outstretched.

"Look, Mama! It's so big!" she squealed, her cheeks flushed with excitement.

"Stay back, Lily!" her mother called, hurrying after her. "Don't touch it, sweetie."

But the girl ignored her mother's warning, placing her small hands on the gingerbread man's leg. For a moment, nothing happened. Then, Clara thought she saw the slightest twitch—a subtle ripple in the dough, as though the gingerbread man had flexed its knee.

Clara blinked, shaking her head. "I'm imagining things," she muttered under her breath.

The little girl giggled and pointed at the gingerbread man's face. "Mama, its eyes are looking at me!"

Her mother grabbed her arm and pulled her back. "Don't be silly. It's just a decoration." But even she hesitated, her eyes narrowing as she glanced up at the figure. "Although... it does look different than before."

Clara stepped forward, her gaze fixed on the gingerbread man. The cranberry eyes, which had seemed bright and cheerful earlier, now glistened darkly, as though something wet and viscous lurked just beneath their surface. The frosting along its mouth had cracked, creating the illusion of jagged teeth.

"Maybe the heat from the lights is causing it to melt," Clara said aloud, though she didn't believe her own words.

As the day wore on, more people began to notice strange changes in the gingerbread man. Its gumdrop buttons, once vibrant and glossy, appeared dull and cracked, as though they'd been bitten into. The intricate frosting patterns on its chest had begun to warp, taking on twisted shapes that seemed almost intentional.

"Is it supposed to look like that?" one man asked, tilting his head as he studied the figure.

"Maybe it's some kind of artistic effect," another woman suggested. "You know, like modern art."

But the whispers in the crowd grew louder, and unease rippled through the square. Clara tried to brush off their comments, but her heart pounded every time she looked at her creation. She couldn't shake the feeling that it was... watching.

By dusk, the square was bathed in the soft glow of lanterns, and the festival was in full swing. Children raced from booth to booth, their laughter ringing out like bells. But then came the scream.

It was high-pitched and panicked, cutting through the noise of the crowd. People turned toward the source, their faces etched with confusion and fear.

"It's Lily!" a woman cried. It was the little girl's mother, her face pale as she frantically searched the crowd. "Has anyone seen my daughter?"

A hush fell over the square as the townsfolk began to look around, calling out Lily's name. Clara's heart sank. She remembered the girl from earlier, the way she had touched the gingerbread man. A terrible thought gripped her.

"She was here just a moment ago," the mother sobbed. "I turned my back for one second—"

"She might have wandered off," the mayor said, trying to calm her. "We'll find her. Everyone spread out and look."

But Clara's gaze was drawn to the gingerbread man. It stood motionless at the center of the square, its cranberry eyes glinting in the lantern light. For a moment, she thought she saw something—a faint outline of a hand pressed against the dough of its leg, as though someone had tried to push their way out.

"No," she whispered, her blood running cold. "That's not possible."

The air grew heavy, the sweet scent of gingerbread becoming cloying and oppressive. Clara took a step closer to the figure, her heart pounding in her ears. She reached out hesitantly, her fingers brushing against its doughy surface. It was warm. Too warm.

"What are you doing?" Mrs. Hannigan's voice cut through the silence, startling Clara. The old woman's face was pale, her expression grim.

"Something's wrong," Clara whispered. "I think... I think it took her."

Mrs. Hannigan's eyes widened, and for a moment, Clara saw raw fear in her gaze. "We need to end this," the old woman said, her voice trembling. "Whatever you've awakened, it won't stop. Not until it's fed."

"What do you mean?" Clara demanded. "What's happening?"

Mrs. Hannigan grabbed her arm, her grip surprisingly strong. "You used the recipe, Clara. The one that binds the golem to the spirit of a child. It's alive, and it's hungry."

Clara's stomach turned. "I didn't mean to—"

"It doesn't matter what you meant!" Mrs. Hannigan snapped. "We have to stop it before it takes another."

But before Clara could respond, a low creaking sound filled the air. It came from the gingerbread man. Slowly, impossibly, its head tilted to the side, the cranberries that served as its eyes glowing faintly in the dim light.

And then it smiled.

Chapter 4: The Baker's Nightmare

The bakery was silent as Clara locked the doors for the night. The festival had ended hours earlier, and the streets outside were dark, blanketed by a thick fog that muted even the sounds of her footsteps. She had stayed late to clean up and organize the kitchen, hoping that the mindless work would distract her from the strange events of the day—the whispers of unease among the townsfolk, the missing child, and, most hauntingly, the way the gingerbread man had seemed to shift its gaze.

"You're just tired," she muttered to herself, her voice echoing in the empty bakery. "It's all in your head."

Yet, as she gathered her things and prepared to head home, a strange unease crept over her. The shadows in the corners of the bakery seemed deeper, and the faint scent of gingerbread lingered in the air, cloying and oppressive. Shaking her head, she flipped off the lights and hurried out the door, trying to ignore the nagging feeling that someone—or something—was watching her.

That night, Clara tossed and turned in bed, unable to find rest. Her mind raced, replaying the events of the day and Mrs. Hannigan's ominous words. When she finally drifted off, her dreams were vivid and terrifying.

She was back in the town square, standing before the giant gingerbread man. The festival lights flickered around her, casting long, eerie shadows. The figure loomed larger than she remembered, its cranberry eyes glowing a deep, unnatural red. The air was thick with the sickly-sweet scent of molasses, making it hard to breathe.

"You shouldn't have made me," a voice rasped, low and gravelly, like the sound of cracking dough. Clara froze, her heart hammering in her chest. The voice seemed to come from everywhere and nowhere at once.

"I didn't mean to," she stammered, her voice barely above a whisper.

The gingerbread man tilted its head, its licorice grin widening to reveal jagged, sugar-coated teeth. "But you did."

Before she could react, the figure lunged, its massive, doughy hand reaching for her. She screamed and turned to run, but her feet wouldn't move. The gingerbread man's fingers closed around her, sticky and impossibly strong. The world spun, and she was dragged into darkness, the scent of gingerbread overwhelming her senses.

Clara jolted awake, gasping for air. Her heart pounded as she sat up, clutching the blankets. Sweat drenched her skin, and her hands trembled as she wiped at her face. It had been a dream, she told herself—a horrible, vivid nightmare. But the fear clung to her, heavy and unshakable.

She glanced at the clock on her nightstand. 3:12 a.m. The room was dark, save for the faint glow of the streetlamp outside her window. She tried to steady her breathing, but something felt... off. The air in the room was heavy, and that same, sickly-sweet scent lingered.

"No," she whispered, shaking her head. "It's just in your head."

But when she swung her legs over the side of the bed, her bare foot brushed something cold and sticky. She yelped and jumped back, fumbling for the lamp. The warm glow illuminated the room, and Clara's stomach dropped.

A smear of frosting stretched across the floor, leading from her bedroom door to the foot of her bed. Bits of crushed gingerbread littered the trail, as though something had been dragged—or had crawled—into the room.

"This isn't happening," Clara whispered, her voice trembling. She stood slowly, careful not to step in the mess, and followed the trail with her eyes. It led out of her bedroom and down the hall.

Clara grabbed the baseball bat she kept by her bed and crept toward the door, every creak of the floorboards making her flinch. She reached the kitchen, flipping on the light, and froze.

The room was a disaster. Flour coated the counters and floor, scattered in chaotic patterns that looked eerily like claw marks. Smears of icing dripped down the walls, and half-crushed gingerbread cookies lay in pieces across the floor, their cheerful frosting faces now twisted into jagged grins.

"No," Clara breathed, her voice shaking. "This isn't real. This can't be real."

Her gaze fell to the center of the room, where a single, massive footprint was pressed into the flour. It was doughy and irregular, with deep indentations where frosting claws might have been. Clara's hands trembled as she stared at the print, her mind racing.

A sudden noise made her spin around, clutching the bat. It was faint, almost imperceptible—a low, wet sound, like the stretching of dough. Her eyes darted to the pantry, where the door stood slightly ajar. The scent of gingerbread was strongest there, thick and suffocating.

Summoning her courage, Clara stepped forward, her grip on the bat tightening. She nudged the door open with the tip of the bat, her breath caught in her throat. The pantry was empty, save for a few scattered baking supplies. But as she turned to leave, she noticed something scrawled on the wall in frosting.

"You can't run from me."

Clara stumbled back, dropping the bat. Her pulse roared in her ears as she fled the kitchen, her mind a whirlwind of fear and disbelief. She locked herself in her bedroom, pushing a dresser against the door, and sat on the floor, clutching her knees to her chest.

It wasn't just a dream. The gingerbread man was real. And it was coming for her.

Chapter 5: The Rise of the Golem

The next morning, Frostwood awoke to an eerie silence. The town square, usually alive with activity during the festival, stood empty. A layer of frost clung to the decorations, and the air carried an unusual stillness, as if the town itself was holding its breath. Clara hurried toward the bakery, her mind racing with the events of the previous night. The trail of frosting, the destroyed kitchen, the threatening message—it all pointed to one horrifying conclusion.

The gingerbread man was alive.

By the time Clara reached the square, a small crowd had gathered around the festival's centerpiece. Whispers rippled through the townsfolk, their eyes fixed on the massive gingerbread figure. Clara pushed her way to the front, her stomach sinking as she took in the sight.

The gingerbread man had changed again. Its once-bright cranberry eyes now glowed faintly, like embers smoldering beneath the surface. The frosting along its mouth had cracked further, exposing jagged "teeth" that seemed sharp enough to bite. The gumdrop buttons on its chest were chipped and fractured, giving it a menacing, battle-worn appearance.

"Did it... move?" someone murmured, their voice tinged with fear.

"It's just the heat from the lights," the mayor said, though his voice wavered. "Nothing to worry about."

Clara's heart pounded as she stepped closer. The air around the gingerbread man felt wrong—thick and heavy, with a sickly-sweet scent that made her stomach churn. She reached out hesitantly, her fingers brushing against its doughy surface. It was warm to the touch.

"It's alive," Clara whispered under her breath. "Oh, God... what have I done?"

Before she could step back, the gingerbread man's head tilted slightly, its glowing eyes locking onto hers. The crowd gasped, some stumbling backward. Clara froze, her mind screaming at her to run, but her feet refused to move.

Then it spoke.

"You," it rasped, its voice low and guttural, like the grinding of sugar against stone. "You brought me back."

The crowd erupted in panicked screams as the gingerbread man's massive arm jerked forward, the motion stiff and unnatural, like a puppet on tangled strings. Its jagged icing claws scraped against the ground, leaving deep gouges in the cobblestone.

"Run!" someone shouted, and the square descended into chaos. People scattered in all directions, pushing and shoving in their desperation to escape.

Clara stumbled backward, her eyes wide with terror. "I didn't mean to," she stammered. "I didn't know—"

The gingerbread man's licorice grin widened, exposing rows of jagged, sugar-coated teeth. "Ignorance does not absolve you," it growled. "I was betrayed. Sacrificed. And now, they will pay."

With a deafening crack, the gingerbread man tore itself free from its base, shards of hardened dough splintering as it stepped forward. The ground trembled beneath its massive weight, and the air filled with the sound of snapping sugar and stretching dough.

Clara turned and ran, her heart pounding in her ears. Behind her, she heard the creature's heavy footsteps, each one accompanied by the crunch of cobblestone beneath its feet. The crowd's screams faded into the distance as she sprinted toward the bakery, her mind racing.

Inside the bakery, Clara slammed the door shut and bolted it, her hands trembling. She leaned against the counter, trying to catch her breath. "What have I done?" she whispered. "How do I stop it?"

The door rattled violently, and Clara yelped, jumping back. For a moment, she thought the creature had followed her, but the knocking was frantic, not heavy. She peeked through the window and saw Mrs. Hannigan outside, her face pale and lined with fear.

Clara unlocked the door and pulled the old woman inside. "It's alive," she said, her voice shaking. "The gingerbread man—it's real."

Mrs. Hannigan nodded grimly. "I told you to leave that recipe alone."

"I didn't know!" Clara cried. "I thought it was just a story!"

"It's more than a story," Mrs. Hannigan said, her voice firm. "That recipe binds the spirit of the betrayed—the child who was sacrificed centuries ago—to the dough. When you baked it, you gave it form. You gave it power."

Clara sank into a chair, her head in her hands. "What do we do? How do we stop it?"

Mrs. Hannigan hesitated, her expression grim. "You can't destroy it. Not while the spirit is bound. But you might be able to weaken it—if you can break the connection to its heart."

"The heart?" Clara asked, looking up. "What do you mean?"

Mrs. Hannigan pointed to the illustration in the recipe book, which Clara had left open on the counter. "The heart is what binds the spirit to the golem. It's the source of its power. Without it, the golem will collapse."

Clara's eyes scanned the page, her heart sinking as she read the description. "The heart is... buried within it," she said, her voice trembling. "How am I supposed to get to it?"

Mrs. Hannigan placed a hand on her shoulder. "You'll have to lure it somewhere you can trap it. Somewhere you can contain it long enough to destroy the heart."

A heavy thud echoed outside, followed by the sound of shattering glass. Clara and Mrs. Hannigan froze, their eyes darting toward the window. The bakery's display case had been smashed, shards of glass littering the ground. Beyond the broken glass, the gingerbread man loomed, its glowing eyes burning like embers.

"You can't hide," it growled, its voice reverberating through the walls. "I will have my vengeance."

Clara's breath caught in her throat. The creature was no longer the charming festival centerpiece she had created. Its limbs were grotesquely twisted, its doughy surface cracked and oozing dark molasses. The jagged frosting claws dripped with a sickly-sweet glaze, and its licorice grin had widened into a nightmarish leer.

Mrs. Hannigan grabbed Clara's arm. "We have to move. Now."

Clara nodded, her fear giving way to a grim determination. She had made this monster, and it was up to her to stop it—before the entire town paid the price.

Chapter 6: Sweet Chaos

The town of Frostwood awoke to a nightmare.

It started quietly, with whispers of strange happenings spreading through the early risers. By mid-morning, those whispers turned to screams. The sweet, comforting scents of baked goods and holiday cheer had twisted into something sinister. The streets, once filled with joy and laughter, now echoed with cries of fear and confusion.

The First Attack

Maggie, the owner of Frostwood's café, was the first to encounter the chaos. She had arrived early to prepare her famous gingerbread muffins for the festival crowd. As the warm scent of cinnamon filled the air, she placed a tray of freshly baked cookies on the counter.

"Perfect as always," she muttered, wiping her hands on her apron.

But as she turned to pour her coffee, a faint rustling caught her attention. She froze, her mug halfway to her lips. The sound came again—like the shuffle of tiny feet.

Her gaze snapped to the tray of cookies. The gingerbread men, which she had painstakingly decorated with smiling faces and candy buttons, were gone.

"What the—?"

Before she could finish her thought, a sharp pain shot through her ankle. She screamed, looking down to see one of her own cookies biting into her leg with jagged, frosting-coated teeth. Its candy eyes glinted with malice as it let out a high-pitched giggle. More cookies swarmed toward her, leaping from the counter with unnatural agility.

Maggie stumbled back, grabbing a rolling pin to defend herself. "Get off me!" she shrieked, swatting at the creatures. The cookies hissed and snarled, their tiny, doughy hands clawing at her.

She ran out of the café, her screams drawing the attention of passersby. The sight of a baker being chased by a swarm of gingerbread men sent the first wave of panic through the town.

The Candy Cane Incident

Across the square, a group of children gathered around a booth selling candy canes. The vendor, an elderly man named Mr. Abbott, handed out the treats with a cheerful smile.

"There you go, kids. Nothing says Christmas like a candy cane!" he said, adjusting his woolen scarf.

But as the children unwrapped their candies, something horrifying happened. The once-innocent treats twisted and warped in their hands, the red and white stripes darkening to blood-red and bone-white. The ends of the candy canes sharpened into vicious points, gleaming in the winter sunlight.

One boy, holding his transformed treat, looked up at Mr. Abbott with wide eyes. "Mister… it's moving."

The candy cane in his hand twitched, then lashed out, slicing across his palm. The boy screamed, dropping the weaponized candy as crimson drops stained the snow. The other children scattered, throwing their candy canes to the ground, but the treats began to writhe like serpents, lunging at anything that moved.

Mr. Abbott grabbed a broom to fend off the rogue candies, but it was no use. One candy cane coiled around his leg, its sharp tip digging into his calf. He cried out, collapsing to the ground as more of the candy canes slithered toward him.

Peppermint Winds

As the chaos spread, a strange wind began to sweep through Frostwood. It carried the overpowering scent of peppermint, which at first seemed pleasant. But the breeze grew stronger, whipping through the streets with unnatural force. Snow swirled in the air, but instead of the usual soft flakes, sharp shards of crystallized sugar sliced through the town.

A group of carolers, huddled together in the square, clutched their coats as the wind howled around them. "What's happening?" one of them shouted, shielding their face from the stinging gusts.

The answer came in the form of a sudden gale that knocked them off their feet. The wind seemed alive, swirling in patterns that formed grotesque faces in the air. The scent of peppermint turned suffocating as the sugary shards cut into exposed skin, leaving tiny, stinging wounds.

The Gingerbread Golem's Wrath

At the center of it all was the Gingerbread Golem, its massive frame casting a shadow over the square. It moved with deliberate purpose, its glowing frosting eyes scanning the chaos with satisfaction. Its voice boomed through the streets, low and guttural, like the grinding of sugar crystals.

"Frostwood betrayed me," it roared. "Now your sweet traditions will turn to bitter vengeance!"

With a swipe of its massive claw, the Golem tore through a booth selling fruitcakes, the dense loaves exploding into a swarm of sticky, flying projectiles. The fruitcakes hurled themselves at fleeing townsfolk, sticking to clothes and skin with a tenacity that made escape nearly impossible.

Across the square, another booth selling hot chocolate erupted in flames as the Golem exhaled a breath of molten molasses. The rich, sticky liquid bubbled and spread, trapping anyone caught in its path like quicksand.

Clara Confronts the Chaos

From the safety of the bakery's upper floor, Clara watched the town descend into madness. Her heart pounded as she saw people running in all directions, pursued by malicious holiday treats. The Golem's booming laughter echoed through the streets, sending chills down her spine.

"We have to do something," Clara said, turning to Mrs. Hannigan.

The old woman's face was grim as she peered out the window. "It's worse than I thought," she said. "The Golem's power is growing. It's not just the spirit of vengeance anymore—it's feeding on the town's fear and chaos."

Clara clenched her fists. "This is my fault. I have to stop it."

Mrs. Hannigan placed a hand on her shoulder. "You can't face it alone, Clara. The Golem is bound to the spirit of the child, and it won't rest until its anger is satisfied. But there's a way to weaken it."

"How?" Clara asked, desperation in her voice.

Mrs. Hannigan gestured to the recipe book on the table. "The same ritual that gave it life can be used to subdue it. But you'll need something powerful to counter its rage—an offering of atonement."

Clara's mind raced. "What kind of offering?"

"One that acknowledges the betrayal," Mrs. Hannigan said. "And one that can release the spirit from its torment."

Clara's eyes filled with determination. "Then tell me what I need to do."

The old woman nodded, her expression resolute. "First, we'll need to gather the ingredients for a binding spell. And second, we'll need to lure the Golem to a place where we can contain it."

As the two women began to prepare, the sounds of chaos outside grew louder. Clara glanced out the window again, her gaze fixed on the towering figure of the Golem. She knew the task ahead would be dangerous, but she couldn't let the town fall to the monster she had created.

"I'm coming for you," she whispered, her voice trembling with both fear and determination. "And this time, I'm going to make it right."

Chapter 7: Secrets in the Dough

Clara sat at the bakery's long wooden table, her hands trembling as she flipped through the brittle pages of the recipe book. The kitchen was eerily silent, save for the occasional groan of the wind outside, carrying the faint cries of townsfolk still fleeing from the Gingerbread Golem's rampage.

Mrs. Hannigan hovered nearby, her face pale and drawn. "That book isn't just a collection of recipes, Clara," she said gravely. "It's a record of Frostwood's darkest secrets."

Clara looked up, her eyes pleading. "You knew, didn't you? About the Golem, about what the town did. Why didn't you warn me?"

Mrs. Hannigan sighed, sinking into a chair. "I tried, Clara. But I never thought anyone would be foolish enough to use that recipe again. Not after what happened the first time."

"What exactly *did* happen?" Clara demanded. "I need to know everything. If I'm going to stop this thing, I have to understand it."

Mrs. Hannigan hesitated, then nodded. "Very well. But it's not an easy story to hear."

The Story of Frostwood's Betrayal

"It was over two hundred years ago," Mrs. Hannigan began. "Frostwood wasn't the charming little town it is today. Back then, it was a harsh and unforgiving place. Winters were brutal, and the townsfolk struggled to survive. When a particularly cruel winter hit, the crops failed, and starvation set in. Desperate to protect what little they had, the town's leaders turned to Margery Grimmel, a baker with knowledge of the old ways—what some would call witchcraft."

Clara leaned forward, her breath catching. "She's the one who made the original Golem."

Mrs. Hannigan nodded. "Yes. Margery believed she could bake a guardian for the town, a creature that would protect them from raiders and wild animals and ensure their survival. But such power comes at a cost. To animate the Golem, she needed more than just flour and spices. She needed a soul."

Clara's stomach twisted. "A soul? Whose soul?"

Mrs. Hannigan's eyes filled with sorrow. "An orphan boy named Elias. He was only seven years old, abandoned by his family and left to fend for himself. The town leaders chose him because they thought no one would miss him."

Clara felt a wave of nausea. "That's... monstrous."

"It was," Mrs. Hannigan agreed. "But the townsfolk were desperate. They convinced themselves it was for the greater good. Margery performed the ritual, binding Elias's spirit to the Golem. At first, it worked. The Golem protected the town, driving off raiders and guarding their food stores. But they underestimated the power of the child's anger and grief."

The Spirit's Wrath

Clara's voice was barely a whisper. "What happened to him?"

"The Golem became unstable," Mrs. Hannigan continued. "Elias's spirit, trapped and tormented, began to lash out. He didn't understand what had happened to him or why he had been sacrificed. The Golem turned on the town, destroying the very people it was meant to protect. It wasn't just rage—it was heartbreak, Clara. He had been betrayed by the only people who could have cared for him."

Clara's hands clenched into fists. "So the town killed him twice. Once when they stole his life, and again when they destroyed the Golem."

Mrs. Hannigan nodded. "They lured it to the edge of the forest and trapped it in a massive kiln. They burned it, hoping to erase their mistake. But Margery warned them it wouldn't be enough. She said the spirit would remain bound as long as the recipe existed—as long as someone had the power to bake it again."

"And now I've brought him back," Clara said, her voice breaking. "I've forced him to relive his nightmare."

Searching for Clues

Clara turned back to the book, flipping through the pages with renewed urgency. She stopped on the recipe for the Gingerbread Golem, her eyes scanning the text. The notes in the margins were cryptic, but one line stood out:

"The heart of the betrayed must be atoned to break the bond."

"The heart," Clara murmured. "It's the key, isn't it? That's what's binding Elias to the Golem."

Mrs. Hannigan nodded. "Yes. The 'heart' is the center of the spell. It's not a physical object—it's the spiritual tether that keeps Elias trapped in the Golem's body."

Clara's mind raced. "If I can break the bond, I can free Elias and stop the Golem. But how do I atone for something that happened centuries ago?"

Mrs. Hannigan pointed to the book. "Margery left instructions, but they're buried in riddles. Look closely—there should be a ritual for atonement somewhere in there."

Clara flipped through the pages, her eyes scanning for anything that resembled a solution. Finally, she found it: **"The Ritual of Release."**

The Ritual of Release

The instructions were fragmented and vague, written in Margery's looping script:

- **Offer sweetness to counter bitterness.**
- **Speak truth to honor betrayal.**
- **Bind intention with a flame of forgiveness.**

"What does it mean?" Clara asked, frustration creeping into her voice. "Offer sweetness? Speak truth? This doesn't tell me anything!"

"It's symbolic," Mrs. Hannigan said. "The sweetness represents the child's stolen innocence. The truth is an acknowledgment of the town's betrayal. And the flame… that's the final act. You'll have to burn the Golem again, but this time with the right intention."

Clara's jaw tightened. "But how do I get close enough to perform the ritual? It's not like the Golem's going to stand still and let me light it on fire."

Mrs. Hannigan's expression darkened. "You'll have to lure it into a trap. Somewhere contained, where it can't escape."

Clara's mind flashed to the bakery's industrial oven—the largest in Frostwood, capable of holding even the monstrous Golem. "The bakery," she said. "We'll lure it here."

A Desperate Plan

Mrs. Hannigan hesitated. "That oven is strong, but it's not indestructible. If this doesn't work, the Golem will destroy the entire building—and us with it."

Clara's gaze hardened. "I don't have a choice. This is my mess. I'm the one who brought him back, and I'm going to fix it."

Mrs. Hannigan nodded slowly. "Very well. But we'll need the right ingredients for the ritual. Sugar and spice alone won't cut it this time."

Clara glanced at the recipe book. "What else do we need?"

Mrs. Hannigan traced a finger over the list in the margin. "Honey for sweetness, to represent the love he was denied. Candied ginger for truth, because it bites but it heals. And salt to purify the bond."

"And the flame?" Clara asked.

Mrs. Hannigan's eyes gleamed. "The flame must come from within. It has to be your intention, Clara. Your will to set him free."

As they gathered the ingredients, Clara's resolve grew. She thought of Elias—an innocent child betrayed and trapped for centuries, his pain twisted into vengeance. She couldn't undo the past, but she could give him peace. And she would stop the Golem, no matter the cost.

The ritual would be dangerous, but it was their only hope. The town had buried its secrets for too long, and now it was time to face the truth.

"Hang on, Elias," Clara whispered as she prepared the mixture. "I'm coming for you."

Chapter 8: The Candied Lair

The town of Frostwood was cloaked in an eerie quiet as Clara and Mrs. Hannigan followed the trail. The air was heavy with the sickly-sweet scent of molasses, and a faint sticky residue coated the ground, leading toward the edge of the forest. Clara's heart pounded in her chest as they neared the abandoned gingerbread house.

"Here," Mrs. Hannigan whispered, stopping abruptly. She pointed ahead, her hand trembling. "This is where it's hiding."

Clara's breath caught as she took in the sight of the gingerbread house. It stood tall and imposing, its walls made of hardened dough, its roof dripping with icing icicles. Candy-cane columns framed the doorway, and gumdrops lined the windowsills. What had once been a festive centerpiece for past festivals now radiated menace. The candy decorations were cracked and discolored, and dark streaks of molasses oozed from between the gingerbread panels like blood from a wound.

"It built this," Clara murmured, horrified. "Out of what?"

Mrs. Hannigan's face was pale. "It used the remains of its victims. Dough, sugar, molasses—fused with flesh and bone. This is no ordinary gingerbread house, Clara. This is its lair."

The Town Discovers the Lair

A small group of townsfolk had gathered behind Clara and Mrs. Hannigan, drawn by whispers of the Golem's hideout. The mayor, pale and visibly shaken, stepped forward. "We have to stop this thing before it destroys the entire town," he said, his voice shaking.

Clara turned to him, her jaw tight. "We're not just dealing with a monster. This is Elias's spirit. It's his rage driving the Golem. Killing it won't solve anything—we need to break the curse."

"And how do you plan to do that?" someone from the crowd asked, their voice laced with fear.

Clara hesitated, her eyes fixed on the ominous house. "I have a plan. But I need to get inside first."

Entering the Lair

Clara stepped forward, clutching the satchel of ingredients she and Mrs. Hannigan had prepared for the ritual. The closer she got to the gingerbread house, the stronger the scent of decay and sugar became. Her boots stuck to the ground with every step, the sticky residue pulling at her feet like tar.

Mrs. Hannigan grabbed her arm. "You don't have to go alone."

Clara shook her head. "I'm the one who brought this thing to life. I need to face it."

The old woman nodded reluctantly. "Be careful, Clara. And remember—Elias isn't your enemy. The curse is."

Clara took a deep breath and pushed open the candy-cane door. It creaked loudly, and the scent of molasses hit her like a wall. She stepped inside, her eyes adjusting to the dim light.

The Twisted Interior

The interior of the gingerbread house was a grotesque parody of holiday cheer. Strings of licorice hung like garlands from the ceiling, but they were stained with dark, sticky streaks. Shattered peppermint shards glittered on the floor like broken glass, and twisted candy canes jutted from the walls like spikes. The entire space was suffused with a faint, pulsing glow, as if the house itself was alive.

Clara's gaze landed on the walls, and her stomach turned. Encased in hardened sugar were the Golem's victims. Their faces were frozen in expressions of terror, their hands outstretched as if reaching for help. The sugary coating glistened in the faint light, preserving them like macabre holiday decorations.

"Oh, my God," Clara whispered, covering her mouth. Her eyes filled with tears as she recognized some of the faces—Maggie, the café owner; Mr. Abbott, the candy vendor; and Lily, the little girl who had gone missing.

She moved deeper into the house, her footsteps crunching on a floor made of crushed candy and cookie crumbs. The walls seemed to close in around her, and the pulsing glow grew stronger.

The Heart of the Lair

At the center of the house, Clara found the source of the glow. A massive cauldron sat in the middle of the room, bubbling with a thick, dark substance that smelled of burnt sugar. The Golem's heart—a pulsating orb of molasses and candy shards—hovered above the cauldron, suspended by strands of sticky licorice. It throbbed with a rhythmic beat, filling the room with an ominous hum.

Clara's hands clenched into fists. "This is it," she murmured. "This is what's binding Elias to the Golem."

Before she could move closer, the ground trembled, and a deep, guttural voice filled the air. "You dare enter my domain?"

Clara whirled around to see the Gingerbread Golem standing in the doorway. Its glowing frosting eyes burned with fury, and its jagged icing claws dripped with molasses. It ducked to enter the room, its massive frame casting a shadow over Clara.

"You," it growled, its voice reverberating through the walls. "You created me. You brought me back."

Clara took a shaky step forward, her heart pounding. "I didn't know," she said, her voice trembling. "I didn't know what the recipe would do. But I know now, Elias. I know what they did to you."

The Golem's grin twisted into a snarl. "They betrayed me. And now, they will suffer."

Clara swallowed hard, her mind racing. "You don't have to do this. I can set you free."

The Golem tilted its head, its eyes narrowing. "Free? There is no freedom. Only vengeance."

A Desperate Escape

The Golem lunged, its massive claws swiping at Clara. She dove to the side, narrowly avoiding the blow. The force of the attack shattered the cauldron, spilling its molten contents across the floor. The room shook violently, chunks of gingerbread and candy falling from the ceiling.

Clara scrambled to her feet, clutching the satchel of ritual ingredients. "Elias, listen to me! I can end this! You don't have to be their weapon anymore!"

The Golem hesitated, its movements slowing. For a brief moment, Clara saw something in its glowing eyes—a flicker of pain, of the boy who had been stolen and betrayed.

"Lies," it growled, though its voice wavered.

Clara took a step closer. "It's not a lie. I know what they did to you. They stole your life, but you don't have to let them define you. Let me help you."

The Golem roared, its voice shaking the walls. But instead of attacking, it turned and stomped out of the house, its massive frame disappearing into the forest.

Clara collapsed to her knees, gasping for breath. The lair trembled around her, the damage from the spilled cauldron causing the structure to collapse. She grabbed the satchel and ran, barely making it out before the gingerbread house crumbled into a pile of sticky debris.

As she stood outside, her chest heaving, she looked back at the ruins. The Golem was gone, but she knew it wasn't over. The heart was still intact, and the ritual still needed to be performed.

"This isn't the end," she whispered. "But now I know what I have to do."

Chapter 9: Fighting Fire with Frosting

The warm glow of the bakery's oven illuminated Clara's face as she frantically sifted through the recipe book. The room was a whirlwind of activity, with jars of spices, bowls of dough, and trays of cookies scattered across every available surface. Clara's hands trembled as she flipped through the brittle pages, searching for inspiration.

"This has to work," she muttered under her breath. The scent of cinnamon and sugar filled the air, masking the lingering smell of burnt molasses that still clung to her from the gingerbread house.

Across the table, Mrs. Hannigan stood silently, her expression grim. She watched as Clara worked, her old hands clutching a mortar and pestle. "You're putting a lot of faith in this plan," she said cautiously. "Enchanted baking is powerful, but it's also unpredictable."

Clara paused, her eyes meeting Mrs. Hannigan's. "I don't have a choice," she said. "I brought the Golem to life with baking, so maybe I can weaken it the same way. If I can't break the curse completely, at least this might buy us enough time to perform the ritual."

Mrs. Hannigan nodded slowly. "What do you need me to do?"

"Help me mix the spices," Clara said, pulling a tattered scrap of parchment from the recipe book. "This calls for cinnamon for protection and powdered sugar for purification. We're going to use these cookies to trap the Golem."

Mrs. Hannigan raised an eyebrow. "Trap it? How?"

Clara held up a sheet of parchment paper where she had sketched a rough design. "The cookies will act as a barrier. If we lay them in the right pattern, they should create a circle of protection strong enough to contain the Golem."

Mrs. Hannigan frowned, but her hands began working with practiced precision, grinding cinnamon sticks into a fine powder. "You're playing with fire, Clara."

"No," Clara said, rolling out a sheet of dough. "I'm fighting fire with frosting."

The Magic of the Cookies

As the night wore on, Clara and Mrs. Hannigan worked tirelessly, mixing, baking, and decorating. Clara infused each batch of cookies with a blend of ingredients carefully chosen for their symbolic properties:

- **Cinnamon** for protection, its warm, spicy scent acting as a ward against malevolent forces.
- **Powdered sugar** for purification, its snowy whiteness representing the cleansing of Elias's corrupted spirit.
- **Honey** for sweetness, a symbol of the innocence stolen from the boy who had been sacrificed.

Each cookie was meticulously shaped and decorated with intricate patterns of frosting. Clara traced symbols of binding and protection onto their surfaces, using food-safe ink made from natural dyes. Her hands ached, and her eyes burned from lack of sleep, but she didn't stop.

"This isn't just baking," she said as she placed another tray into the oven. "It's crafting magic."

Mrs. Hannigan nodded, sprinkling a final layer of powdered sugar over a batch of cooled cookies. "Be careful with your intentions, Clara. Every spell has consequences."

"I know," Clara replied, pulling the tray from the oven. The cookies glistened as if imbued with their own inner light. "But this isn't about destruction. It's about protection—and redemption."

The Plan Comes Together

By dawn, the bakery was filled with dozens of cookies, each one a tiny masterpiece. Clara arranged them into boxes, carefully layering them with wax paper to prevent breakage. She pulled out a map of the town square and began sketching a pattern on the parchment.

"We'll place the cookies in a protective circle around the Golem," Clara explained to Mrs. Hannigan. "The cinnamon and sugar will create a barrier it can't cross, and the symbols will weaken its connection to the curse."

Mrs. Hannigan squinted at the map. "And how do you plan to lure it into the circle?"

Clara hesitated. "I'm going to bait it."

Mrs. Hannigan's eyes widened. "You can't be serious."

"I am," Clara said firmly. "It's after me, Mrs. Hannigan. I'm the one who brought it back, and I'm the one it blames. If I lead it into the trap, it'll follow."

"That's reckless, Clara," Mrs. Hannigan said. "What if it doesn't work? What if it catches you before you can complete the circle?"

Clara's jaw tightened. "I'll have to be faster."

Setting the Trap

The sun was rising as Clara and Mrs. Hannigan carried the boxes of enchanted cookies to the town square. The streets were deserted, the townsfolk hiding in their homes after the previous night's chaos. Clara could feel the weight of their fear as she laid the cookies in a wide circle, carefully placing each one in the exact position dictated by her diagram.

"Are you sure this will work?" Mrs. Hannigan asked, placing the last cookie.

"It has to," Clara said, standing back to examine the completed circle. The cookies formed a perfect barrier, their frosted symbols glowing faintly in the morning light. "Now all we need is the Golem."

Mrs. Hannigan handed her a small pouch of cinnamon and powdered sugar. "If it tries to cross the circle, throw this at it. It should amplify the barrier."

Clara nodded, clutching the pouch tightly. "Thank you."

Mrs. Hannigan grabbed her arm. "Don't thank me yet. Just... come back alive, Clara."

Luring the Golem

Clara stood in the center of the square, her heart pounding as she called out into the stillness. "Elias! I'm here!"

Her voice echoed through the empty streets. For a moment, there was only silence. Then, the ground began to tremble.

The Gingerbread Golem emerged from the shadows, its massive frame filling the narrow street as it lumbered toward the square. Its glowing frosting eyes burned with rage, and its jagged icing claws dripped with molten molasses. The sweet scent of gingerbread was overpowering, but it carried an undercurrent of rot.

"You," it growled, its voice reverberating through the air. "You cannot escape me."

Clara stood her ground, her hands trembling but her resolve unshaken. "I'm not running," she said. "But you don't have to do this, Elias. I can set you free."

The Golem laughed, a deep, rumbling sound that shook the buildings around them. "Lies. You seek to destroy me, as they did before."

"I don't want to destroy you," Clara said, backing slowly toward the circle. "I want to help you."

The Golem followed, its massive feet cracking the cobblestone. As Clara crossed into the circle, she felt the faint hum of energy from the cookies. The Golem stepped forward, but the moment its foot touched the barrier, it recoiled with a roar of pain.

"What is this?" it snarled, swiping at the cookies with its claws. But the barrier held, the cinnamon and powdered sugar sizzling like fire against its doughy skin.

Clara threw the contents of the pouch at the Golem, the powder creating a shimmering cloud that surrounded it. The creature thrashed, its movements growing sluggish as the enchanted cookies began to weaken its connection to the curse.

"No!" it roared, its voice tinged with desperation. "You will not bind me!"

Clara's heart ached as she watched the Golem struggle. "I'm not trying to bind you, Elias," she said softly. "I'm trying to set you free."

The Golem let out a final, ear-splitting roar as it collapsed to its knees, its massive frame trembling. The barrier held firm, and for the first time, Clara felt a glimmer of hope.

"Now," she whispered, clutching the ritual ingredients. "It's time to end this."

Chapter 10: The Sweet Reckoning

The town square was bathed in an eerie glow, the enchanted circle of cookies pulsing faintly as Clara stood at its center. The Gingerbread Golem loomed just outside the protective barrier, its massive, doughy body steaming with rage. Its glowing frosting eyes flickered, casting sharp shadows across the cobblestones. Clara's heart pounded as she clutched the ritual ingredients, her fingers trembling.

The crowd of townsfolk who had gathered around the square watched in terrified silence. Among them were the mayor, Maggie the café owner, and even a few teenagers who had decided to stay and fight. Each carried makeshift weapons—rolling pins, iron skillets, and bags of salt—but their fear was palpable.

"This thing is getting stronger," Clara said, her voice strained as she turned to Mrs. Hannigan. "Every time it attacks, it feeds on fear and chaos. If we don't finish this soon, it'll break free."

Mrs. Hannigan nodded grimly. "Then we need to hold it here. The longer it stays inside the circle, the weaker it will become."

The Battle Begins

The Golem growled, pacing just beyond the circle, its claws scraping against the cobblestones with a sound like grinding sugar. "You think your little tricks can stop me?" it boomed, its voice reverberating through the square. "I am vengeance! I am betrayal! And I will consume you all!"

Clara swallowed hard and took a step forward. "You're more than that, Elias," she said, her voice steady despite her fear. "You're a child who was wronged, but you don't have to let their betrayal define you."

The Golem's glowing eyes narrowed, and for a moment, it hesitated. But the flicker of recognition was short-lived. With a deafening roar, it swiped at the barrier, its claws colliding with an explosion of sparks as the enchanted cookies held firm. The ground shook, and several townsfolk stumbled back.

"Hold your ground!" Clara shouted, her voice cutting through the chaos. She turned to the group. "We have to keep it distracted while I perform the ritual. Keep it focused on us, but don't let it cross the circle!"

Maggie stepped forward, brandishing her rolling pin like a sword. "You heard her! Let's show this overgrown cookie who's boss!"

The townsfolk rallied, hurling salt and flour at the Golem as it continued to batter the barrier. Every attack sent shocks through the circle, but the enchanted cookies absorbed the energy, their symbols glowing brighter with each strike.

The Golem Grows Stronger

As the battle wore on, the Golem seemed to adapt. Its attacks became more precise, its claws slicing through the air with deadly speed. With every strike, cracks began to form in the protective circle. Clara's chest tightened as she realized the barrier wouldn't hold much longer.

"This isn't working," she said, turning to Mrs. Hannigan. "We're running out of time."

Mrs. Hannigan's gaze was fixed on the Golem. "Then it's time to use the replica."

Clara hesitated. The replica—a gingerbread child she had baked earlier—was her last resort. It had been crafted with care, using the same enchanted ingredients as the cookies in the barrier. Its design was simple but unmistakable: a small, innocent figure meant to resemble Elias.

"It's risky," Clara said. "If it doesn't recognize the replica, it could make things worse."

Mrs. Hannigan placed a hand on Clara's shoulder. "Trust in the magic. And trust in him."

Facing the Replica

Clara took a deep breath and retrieved the gingerbread child from her satchel. The townsfolk fell silent as she stepped forward, holding the small figure out in front of her. The Golem froze mid-attack, its glowing eyes narrowing as it focused on the replica.

"What is this?" it growled, its voice low and dangerous.

"It's you, Elias," Clara said softly. "It's what you used to be before they took everything from you. Look at it. Remember who you were."

The Golem hesitated, its massive form trembling. Its eyes flickered, the glowing light dimming as it stared at the gingerbread child. For a moment, the air was heavy with silence, and Clara saw something shift in the creature's expression—a flicker of sorrow, of recognition.

"I... was this?" the Golem rasped, its voice softer now. "I was... innocent."

"Yes," Clara said, stepping closer. "And they betrayed you. But you don't have to carry that pain forever. Let me help you let go."

The Golem's claws lowered, its massive frame slumping as it gazed at the replica. "I... don't know how."

The Final Ritual

Clara moved quickly, placing the replica at the center of the circle. She poured the mixture of honey, cinnamon, and powdered sugar over it, her hands steady as she recited the incantation from the recipe book:

"Sweetness to heal, truth to honor, fire to release. Let the chains of bitterness dissolve, and the spirit find peace."

The air around her shimmered, the symbols on the cookies glowing brightly as the ritual took effect. The Golem let out a low, mournful sound, its massive body trembling as cracks began to form across its surface.

"No," it whispered, its voice laced with both fear and relief. "What... is happening?"

"You're being set free," Clara said, her voice firm but kind. "It's time to rest, Elias."

The Golem's End

The Golem let out one final roar, a sound that echoed with centuries of pain and anger. Its massive body began to crumble, pieces of dough and icing falling away like ash. The glowing light in its eyes faded, replaced by a soft, golden glow that radiated peace.

As the last remnants of the Golem dissolved, the replica at the center of the circle glowed brightly, then faded into nothingness. The square fell silent, the oppressive energy lifting like a fog.

Clara sank to her knees, her chest heaving as she tried to catch her breath. Around her, the townsfolk began to cheer, their fear giving way to relief.

"You did it," Mrs. Hannigan said, kneeling beside her. "You set him free."

Clara nodded, tears streaming down her face. "It's over."

Aftermath

The next morning, the town square was filled with light and laughter once again. The air was crisp and clean, free of the heavy sweetness that had lingered for days. The enchanted cookies were gone, their magic spent, but the memory of their power remained.

Clara stood in front of the bakery, watching as the townsfolk began to rebuild. Though the battle had left scars, there was a sense of hope in the air—a belief that Frostwood could move forward.

Mrs. Hannigan joined her, placing a hand on her shoulder. "You did something incredible, Clara. You didn't just save the town—you gave Elias the peace he deserved."

Clara smiled faintly, her gaze fixed on the horizon. "I just hope he's finally free."

And for the first time in days, the air felt lighter, as if a great weight had been lifted from the world. The Gingerbread Golem was gone, but its story would live on—a reminder of the power of forgiveness, and the strength it takes to confront the past.

Chapter 11: A Bittersweet Truth

The morning after the battle in the town square, Frostwood awoke to an uneasy calm. The Gingerbread Golem was gone, its wrath dissolved into the night, but Clara couldn't shake the lingering weight in her chest. Though the town had survived, she knew the curse wasn't truly broken. Not yet.

She sat in the bakery's back room, the tattered recipe book open in front of her. Its brittle pages were marked with cryptic notes and symbols, each one whispering of secrets long buried. Mrs. Hannigan sat across from her, stirring a steaming mug of tea as she watched Clara's furrowed brow.

"You're thinking too hard," Mrs. Hannigan said finally. "It's over, Clara. You freed Elias."

Clara shook her head. "Not completely. I can feel it—like there's still something unfinished. The ritual weakened the curse, but it didn't destroy it. The recipe still exists, and so does the pain tied to it."

Mrs. Hannigan sighed. "The town buried its guilt long ago. The curse isn't just in the book—it's in Frostwood itself. Until we confront what really happened, the curse will linger."

Uncovering the Truth

Determined to find answers, Clara spent the day digging through Frostwood's archives. The town library, dusty and neglected, held records that stretched back to its founding. She poured over brittle documents and faded ledgers, piecing together the story of Elias's sacrifice.

In the margins of an old journal belonging to one of the town's founders, she found the confirmation she'd been dreading. The words were scrawled in a shaky hand, as though the writer couldn't bear to record them:

"We took his innocence. We took his life. The boy was sweet as honey, but we turned him bitter as ash. We buried him in the woods, beneath the sugar maple, and prayed he'd forgive us. But how can a soul forgive when no one remembers his name?"

Clara's stomach twisted as she read the words. She slammed the journal shut and turned to Mrs. Hannigan, who had followed her to the library. "They knew," Clara said, her voice shaking. "They knew what they did was wrong, but they hid it. They buried the boy like he was nothing. No wonder he couldn't rest."

Mrs. Hannigan placed a hand on Clara's shoulder. "Then you know what you have to do."

Clara nodded, determination hardening her expression. "We have to honor him. We have to make the town remember."

Confronting the Town

That evening, Clara stood in the town square, the journal clutched tightly in her hands. The townsfolk had gathered, drawn by whispers of her discovery. They murmured among themselves, their faces a mix of curiosity and unease.

"What's this about, Clara?" the mayor asked, stepping forward. His usually confident demeanor was tinged with nervousness.

Clara took a deep breath and held up the journal. "This is the truth about Elias," she said, her voice carrying across the square. "The boy who became the Gingerbread Golem. The boy who was sacrificed so the town could survive."

A gasp rippled through the crowd, followed by uneasy whispers.

"What are you talking about?" Maggie asked, her voice shaking. "That's just a story, isn't it?"

"No," Clara said firmly. "It's real. The founders of Frostwood took a child—a sweet, innocent boy—and bound his soul to a magical ritual. They made him a guardian, but when the ritual went wrong, they killed him again. They buried him and erased his name from history."

The crowd fell silent, the weight of her words settling over them like a heavy fog.

"This town owes him," Clara continued, her voice steady. "We owe him an apology, a memorial, and the truth. We can't keep hiding from what happened."

Creating the Memorial

The townsfolk, shaken but resolute, joined Clara in the woods. They followed her to the sugar maple mentioned in the journal, its gnarled roots twisting over the ground like skeletal fingers. The air was thick with an almost tangible energy, as though the land itself was waiting.

Clara knelt by the tree, placing a small bundle of baked offerings at its base. She had spent the afternoon crafting them—a dozen gingerbread children, each one delicately decorated to honor Elias's memory. She sprinkled the cookies with powdered sugar and honey, whispering a quiet prayer for forgiveness.

Mrs. Hannigan stepped forward with a wooden plaque, which the townsfolk had engraved with care:

In Memory of Elias:
A Boy Taken Too Soon.
May His Spirit Rest in Sweet Peace.

The mayor read the inscription aloud, his voice breaking. "We were wrong," he said, addressing the crowd. "The founders made a terrible mistake, and we've all lived under the weight of their choices. It's time to make amends."

As the plaque was mounted at the base of the tree, Clara lit a small candle and placed it among the cookies. The flame flickered, casting a warm glow that seemed to spread outward, enveloping the clearing in a soft, golden light.

The Curse Unravels

A low hum filled the air, and the ground beneath the tree trembled. Clara stepped back, her heart pounding as the energy around them intensified. The branches of the sugar maple shivered, their leaves rustling with a sound like whispers.

Then, from the base of the tree, a soft golden light emerged. It swirled upward, taking the shape of a small boy. His form was delicate and shimmering, like sunlight reflected on water. He had wide, innocent eyes and a shy smile, and his presence filled the air with a bittersweet warmth.

"Elias," Clara whispered, tears streaming down her face.

The boy's gaze swept over the crowd, his expression a mix of curiosity and sadness. "You remember me?" he asked, his voice soft and trembling.

"We do," Clara said, stepping forward. "We're sorry for what happened to you. You deserved better."

The boy's form flickered, and a single tear rolled down his cheek. "I was so lonely," he said. "I didn't understand why they hurt me."

Clara knelt before him, her voice steady but full of emotion. "You didn't deserve their betrayal, Elias. But we're here now, and we won't forget you again."

The boy's smile grew, and the golden light around him intensified. "Thank you," he whispered.

As the light grew brighter, Elias's form began to dissolve, scattering into a million tiny sparks that floated upward into the night sky. The oppressive energy that had hung over Frostwood lifted, replaced by a sense of peace.

A Town Changed

The next morning, the sugar maple stood taller, its branches fuller and its bark glistening with dew. The plaque at its base shone brightly, and the scent of honey and cinnamon lingered in the air.

Clara stood with Mrs. Hannigan, watching as the townsfolk visited the memorial. Some left flowers, others lit candles, and a few placed small offerings of gingerbread and sugar.

"You did it," Mrs. Hannigan said, her voice filled with pride.

Clara shook her head. "We did it. The whole town did. And now Elias can finally rest."

As the two women turned to leave, Clara glanced back at the tree one last time. A faint golden glow shimmered in its branches, like a final goodbye.

It was a bittersweet truth, but it was the truth—and for the first time in centuries, Frostwood was free.

Chapter 12: Crumbs of the Past

The weeks after the Gingerbread Golem's defeat were a flurry of activity in Frostwood. The town, though battered and scarred, slowly began to rebuild. Streets that had been cracked and coated in sticky molasses were scrubbed clean, storefronts shattered by the Golem's rampage were repaired, and the laughter of children returned to the town square.

Clara stood in the bakery one brisk morning, watching as customers trickled in and out, their faces brighter than they had been in days. The air carried the warm scent of freshly baked goods, but it also carried something deeper—a fragile hope. The curse was broken, or so everyone believed, and for the first time in years, Frostwood seemed to breathe freely.

"Morning, Clara!" Maggie, the café owner, called as she entered the bakery. "Got any more of those cranberry muffins? My customers are asking for them nonstop."

Clara smiled, wiping her hands on her apron. "Coming right up. I made a fresh batch this morning."

As she placed the muffins into a box, Maggie leaned closer. "You've done a lot for this town, Clara. People are saying you're a hero."

Clara chuckled softly. "I'm no hero. I just cleaned up a mess I helped create."

Maggie gave her a knowing look. "Maybe, but you still saved us. Don't forget that."

The Lingering Scars

Despite the town's optimism, the scars left by the curse were undeniable. The sugar maple memorial had become a focal point for the community, a place where people left offerings and lit candles in Elias's memory. Yet, the older townsfolk whispered about the past in hushed tones, their voices heavy with guilt.

Clara often visited the memorial, drawn to its quiet presence. The tree stood tall and strong, its branches casting dappled shadows over the plaque that bore Elias's name. Beneath it sat the replica gingerbread child Clara had baked—a symbol of innocence and remembrance. Its frosted smile had become a comforting sight to many.

But not to Clara.

A Growing Unease

One crisp evening, Clara stood alone at the memorial, a steaming cup of tea warming her hands. The sun dipped below the horizon, painting the sky in hues of orange and pink. The sugar maple's leaves rustled gently in the breeze, but there was something in the air that made Clara's skin prickle.

She stepped closer to the gingerbread child, her brow furrowing. Its frosting seemed... different. The once-smooth surface of its decorations now bore faint cracks, as if the dough beneath was drying out. Clara knelt, running her fingers over the frosting.

"It's probably just the weather," she murmured to herself, but the words rang hollow. She had used enchanted ingredients to make the replica—ingredients that shouldn't decay.

A faint scent wafted up, one that sent a chill down her spine. It was the unmistakable aroma of ginger and molasses, but it was sharper now, tinged with something bitter. Something wrong.

Clara stood quickly, her pulse quickening. "No," she whispered. "It's over. It has to be over."

A Chilling Discovery

The next day, Clara returned to the memorial with Mrs. Hannigan. Together, they examined the gingerbread child, their expressions growing darker with each passing moment.

"These cracks shouldn't be here," Clara said, her voice tight. "I sealed it perfectly."

Mrs. Hannigan knelt beside her, her eyes narrowing. "It's not just the cracks," she said, scraping a bit of the frosting with her fingernail. The substance beneath was darker than it should have been, almost black, and it gave off that same sharp, sinister scent.

"What does it mean?" Clara asked, though she already suspected the answer.

Mrs. Hannigan hesitated, then stood with a sigh. "It means the curse isn't entirely gone. Something of Elias's pain, his anger... it's still tied to this place."

Clara's stomach churned. "But the ritual—"

"The ritual gave him peace," Mrs. Hannigan interrupted, her tone firm. "But it didn't erase what was done. The past doesn't disappear, Clara. It lingers, like crumbs scattered on a table."

The Twist

That night, Clara couldn't sleep. She sat in her kitchen, staring at the recipe book that had caused so much destruction. She had kept it locked away, swearing to herself that she'd never use it again. But now, with the cracks in the replica and the scent of ginger haunting her, she couldn't ignore the nagging feeling that the book still held answers.

She opened it, her fingers trembling as she flipped through the pages. When she reached the recipe for the Gingerbread Golem, her breath caught. The ink on the page seemed darker than before, the letters more vivid, as though the book had come alive. And at the bottom of the page, a line of text had appeared that hadn't been there before:

"In sweetness lies sorrow, and in sorrow lies strength. The past is never truly buried."

Clara slammed the book shut, her heart racing. She grabbed it and ran to the sugar maple, where the gingerbread child sat beneath the tree. The cracks in its frosting had deepened, and the faint golden glow that had surrounded it after the ritual was now gone.

"No," Clara whispered, kneeling before the replica. "This can't be happening."

A cold wind swept through the clearing, carrying with it the sharp scent of ginger and molasses. The leaves of the sugar maple rustled violently, and for a moment, Clara thought she heard a whisper—a child's voice, soft and mournful.

"Remember me..."

She stumbled back, her hands shaking. The whisper was faint, but it was enough to send chills down her spine. The replica's cracked frosting seemed to shift in the dim light, its once-sweet smile twisting into something darker.

A Haunting Reminder

Clara fled back to the bakery, her mind racing. As she locked the doors and sat in the silence of the kitchen, she realized the truth: the curse might never fully be gone. Elias's pain, the betrayal of the town—it had left a mark too deep to erase entirely.

She stared at the recipe book, now resting on the counter. It seemed to hum with a faint energy, as though waiting for the right moment to awaken again.

As she turned out the lights and headed upstairs, the scent of ginger lingered in the air. It wasn't overwhelming, but it was there—subtle and sinister, like a shadow waiting in the corner.

And somewhere in the darkened town, beneath the sugar maple, a faint crack echoed through the night.

Message from the Author:

I hope you enjoyed this book, I love astrology and knew there was not a book such as this out on the shelf. I love metaphysical items as well. Please check out my other books:

-Life of Government Benefits

-My life of Hell

-My life with Hydrocephalus

-Red Sky

-World Domination:Woman's rule

-World Domination:Woman's Rule 2: The War

-Life and Banishment of Apophis: book 1

-The Kidney Friendly Diet

-The Ultimate Hemp Cookbook

-Creating a Dispensary(legally)

-Cleanliness throughout life: the importance of showering from childhood to adulthood.

-Strong Roots: The Risks of Overcoddling children

-Hemp Horoscopes: Cosmic Insights and Earthly Healing

- Celestial Hemp Navigating the Zodiac: Through the Green Cosmos

-Astrological Hemp: Aligning The Stars with Earth's Ancient Herb

-The Astrological Guide to Hemp: Stars, Signs, and Sacred Leaves

-Green Growth: Innovative Marketing Strategies for your Hemp Products and Dispensary

-Cosmic Cannabis

-Astrological Munchies

-Henry The Hemp

-Zodiacal Roots: The Astrological Soul Of Hemp

- **Green Constellations: Intersection of Hemp and Zodiac**

-Hemp in The Houses: An astrological Adventure Through The Cannabis Galaxy

-Galactic Ganja Guide

Heavenly Hemp

Zodiac Leaves

Doctor Who Astrology

Cannastrology

Stellar Satvias and Cosmic Indicas

Celestial Cannabis: A Zodiac Journey

AstroHerbology: The Sky and The Soil: Volume 1

AstroHerbology:Celestial Cannabis:Volume 2

Cosmic Cannabis Cultivation

The Starry Guide to Herbal Harmony: Volume 1

The Starry Guide to Herbal Harmony: Cannabis Universe: Volume 2

Yugioh Astrology: Astrological Guide to Deck, Duels and more

Nightmare Mansion: Echoes of The Abyss

Nightmare Mansion 2: Legacy of Shadows

Nightmare Mansion 3: Shadows of the Forgotten

Nightmare Mansion 4: Echoes of the Damned

The Life and Banishment of Apophis: Book 2

Nightmare Mansion: Halls of Despair

Healing with Herb: Cannabis and Hydrocephalus

Planetary Pot: Aligning with Astrological Herbs: Volume 1

Fast Track to Freedom: 30 Days to Financial Independence Using AI, Assets, and Agile Hustles

Cosmic Hemp Pathways

How to Become Financially Free in 30 Days: 10,000 Paths to Prosperity

Zodiacal Herbage: Astrological Insights: Volume 1

Nightmare Mansion: Whispers in the Walls

The Daleks Invade Atlantis

Henry the hemp and Hydrocephalus

10X The Kidney Friendly Diet

Cannabis Universe: Adult coloring book

Hemp Astrology: The Healing Power of the Stars

Zodiacal Herbage: Astrological Insights: Cannabis Universe: Volume 2

Planetary Pot: Aligning with Astrological Herbs: Cannabis Universes: Volume 2

Doctor Who Meets the Replicators and SG-1: The Ultimate Battle for Survival

Nightmare Mansion: Curse of the Blood Moon

The Celestial Stoner: A Guide to the Zodiac

Cosmic Pleasures: Sex Toy Astrology for Every Sign

Hydrocephalus Astrology: Navigating the Stars and Healing Waters

Lapis and the Mischievous Chocolate Bar

Celestial Positions: Sexual Astrology for Every Sign

Apophis's Shadow Work Journal: **:** A Journey of Self-Discovery and Healing

Kinky Cosmos: Sexual Kink Astrology for Every Sign

Digital Cosmos: The Astrological Digimon Compendium

Stellar Seeds: The Cosmic Guide to Growing with Astrology

Apophis's Daily Gratitude Journal

Cat Astrology: Feline Mysteries of the Cosmos

The Cosmic Kama Sutra: An Astrological Guide to Sexual Positions

Unleash Your Potential: A Guided Journal Powered by AI Insights

Whispers of the Enchanted Grove

Cosmic Pleasures: An Astrological Guide to Sexual Kinks

369, 12 Manifestation Journal

Whisper of the nocturne journal(blank journal for writing or drawing)

The Boogey Book

Locked In Reflection: A Chastity Journey Through Locktober

Generating Wealth Quickly:

How to Generate $100,000 in 24 Hours

Star Magic: Harness the Power of the Universe

The Flatulence Chronicles: A Fart Journal for Self-Discovery

The Doctor and The Death Moth

Seize the Day: A Personal Seizure Tracking Journal

The Ultimate Boogeyman Safari: A Journey into the Boogie World and Beyond

Whispers of Samhain: 1,000 Spells of Love, Luck, and Lunar Magic: Samhain Spell Book

Apophis's guides:

Witch's Spellbook Crafting Guide for Halloween

Frost & Flame: The Enchanted Yule Grimoire of 1000 Winter Spells

The Ultimate Boogey Goo Guide & Spooky Activities for Halloween Fun

Harmony of the Scales: A Libra's Spellcraft for Balance and Beauty

The Enchanted Advent: 36 Days of Christmas Wonders

Nightmare Mansion: The Labyrinth of Screams

Harvest of Enchantment: 1,000 Spells of Gratitude, Love, and Fortune for Thanksgiving

The Boogey Chronicles: A Journal of Nightly Encounters and Shadowy Secrets

The 12 Days of Financial Freedom: A Step-by-Step Christmas Countdown to Transform Your Finances

Sigil of the Eternal Spiral Blank Journal

A Christmas Feast: Timeless Recipes for Every Meal

Cosmic Sales: The Astrological Guide to Black Friday Shopping
Legends of the Corn Mother and Other Harvest Myths
Whispers of the Harvest: The Corn Mother's Journal
The Evergreen Spellbook
The Doctor Meets the Boogeyman
The White Witch of Rose Hall's SpellBook
The Gingerbread Golem's Shadow: A Study in Sweet Darkness
The Gingerbread Golem Codex: An Academic Exploration of Sweet Myths
The Gingerbread Golem Grimoire: Sweet Magicks and Spells for the Festive Witch

If you want solar for your home go here: https://www.harborsolar.live/apophisenterprises/

Get Some Tarot cards: https://www.makeplayingcards.com/sell/apophis-occult-shop

Get some shirts: https://www.bonfire.com/store/apophis-shirt-emporium/

Instagrams:
@apophis_enterprises,
@apophisbookemporium,
@apophisscardshop
Twitter: @apophisenterpr1
 Tiktok:@apophisenterprise
Youtube: @sg1fan23477, @FiresideRetreatKingdom
Hive: @sg1fan23477
CheeLee: @SG1fan23477

Podcast: Apophis Chat Zone: https://open.spotify.com/show/
5zXbrCLEV2xzCp8ybrfHsk?si=fb4d4fdbdce44dec

Newsletter: https://apophiss-newsletter-27c897.beehiiv.com/

Milton Keynes UK
Ingram Content Group UK Ltd.
UKHW022334041224
452010UK00019B/1142

9 798330 611942